apples

 butter

 clock

 cookbook

 cookies

 cupboard

 cupcakes

 flour

 lemon

 pie

 ponies

 recipe

 ribbon

 sugar

 sun

The Missing Recipe

by Ruth Benjamin

illustrated by Angel Rodriguez

HarperFestival®

A Division of HarperCollins*Publishers*

The Ponyville baking

contest was this afternoon.

Sweetberry planned to

bake her best .

Sweetberry looked

for her  .

She looked in the  .

She looked in the  .

Where could it be?

she wondered.

"Do you want to come out

and play?" asked Cupcake.

"The  is shining."

"Yes," said Sweetberry.

"But first I must find my

 .

It is missing!"

"I will help you!"

said Cupcake.

They looked all over

for the  .

They did not find it.

How would Sweetberry

make her  ?

"I have an idea!" said

Sweetberry.

"I will make a new type of

 —without a

I will mix , ,

and  for the

 crust."

"I will cut for the  filling," said

Sweetberry.

"I will mix the with juice and ."

Cupcake looked at

the  .

"I have to go now," she said.

"I am making  for the

baking contest."

"Thanks for helping me," said

Sweetberry.

Sweetberry put the  in the oven.

"Wow!" she said.

"There is my

.

It is stuck to the bag of

."

"It is too late to bake a new  now,"

said Sweetberry.

Just then she realized—

she had made a yummy

 without any

at all!

Sweetberry giggled.

There were so many treats

at the baking contest.

Minty had baked

and Cupcake had

baked  .

But all of the

lined up for a taste of

Sweetberry's  .

Sweetberry won the

 for best .

She felt proud.

"Trying new things feels

good," she told the .

They ate the rest of the

 together.